Jitters
in the
Jungle

Noel Ward

Illustrations Terry Myler

THE CHILDREN'S PRESS

For
Rory and Carmel

First published 2002 by
The Children's Press
an imprint of Anvil Books
45 Palmerston Road, Dublin 6

2 4 6 8 7 5 3 1

© Text Noel Ward 2002
© Illustrations Terry Myler 2002

ISBN 1 901737 42 X

Typeset by Computertype Limited
Printed by Colour Books Limited

Contents

1 Mitch and Me

It was morning at the Swinging Vine Health and Fitness Club.

The fearless fighter Knuckles Neddy the Elephant – that's me – was busy working out. I needed to.

Next week I was to fight Cool Vinny the Lion.

Not just any old fight.

Up for grabs was the Heavy-weight Boxing Title of the Deep Dark Jungle.

4

Things weren't going too well.

In fact, they were going badly.

This morning my manager, Mitch the Chimp, had asked me to practise my shadow-boxing. The shadow had won hands down!

I'M FINISHED

Now I was hanging, panting, against the ropes of the boxing-ring. Sweat was rolling down my trunk.

'Me and the fight game is finished, Mitch,' I croaked. 'I'm hanging up the gloves. I'm no good any more.'

Mitch flew into a rage.

'Whaddaya mean, you wanna quit?'
he fumed. 'In a week, you're taking
on Cool Vinny in the biggest fight
this jungle has ever seen.'

I didn't need reminding. Behind
us in the gym was a poster. Dozens
were plastered all over the jungle.

I could hardly bear to look at it.

It's the Greatest!

THE MOTHER OF ALL FIGHTS!

COOL VINNY
V
KNUCKLES NEDDY!

Be there for the show-down!

Cool Vinny was the toughest,
angriest, and generally baddest beast
in the Deep Dark Jungle.

Any animal who got into a boxing-ring with him came out with a lot less teeth and not a lot of fur.

He ripped up palm trees just for fun. That was when they were big. When they were small he used them as toothpicks to clean his teeth with.

He was that kind of lion.

And I, who couldn't even beat my own shadow, was to fight him. I would have to tell Mitch there was no way I was getting into that ring.

'Listen, Mitch...' I began. I would have to give *some* excuse. 'I can't do it...I can't stand the thought of hitting poor little animals any more.'

'Cool Vinny! A poor little animal, my foot!' Mitch stormed. 'You don't like the thought of other animals hitting *you*. You've gone soft!'

It was true and I knew it. I was not as tough as I used to be. I sat slumped on a stool in the corner of the ring, trying not to cry.

I was not only sorry for myself. I was sorry for Mitch too. He and I had been friends for ever. He had never insisted on my fighting when I didn't want to.

Now, however, he had a problem on his mind. A real big problem.

You see, Mitch was a gambler. First he used to bet on the boxers he managed. This wasn't a good idea because his boxers didn't always box as well as they should have. In fact, most of them boxed as well as Mitch managed them – which was poorly.

Then he began to gamble with Big Sid the Crocodile, the nastiest gangster in the jungle. That was an equally dumb steer. Now he owed Big Sid a stack.

He had tried his hardest to raise it. Coffee mornings. Sales of work. It wasn't enough.

So yesterday he had put everything he had on the 3.30 at the Tic-Tac Track. On Ollie O the ostrich, the fastest bird in the jungle.

Unfortunately, Ollie O got his legs in a twist at the start of the race and never got going.

So Mitch really needed that fight money to pay off Big Sid.

I was wavering. Should I chance it? I knew Cool Vinny had a weak spot in his neck. Maybe I could knock him out. It would have to be at the start. I'd never make it to Round 2.

'Mitch...' I began. Then I stopped.

'Hiya, boys,' hissed a voice.

2 Big Sid

It was Big Sid! Did I say he was a
nasty guy? You can put icing on that.

'B...Bi...Big Sid,' I stuttered, seeing
that Mitch was speechless. 'This is a
nice surprise.'

'Beat it, chump,' Big Sid hissed.
'It's your high-flying friend I want to
talk to.'

'You've been avoiding me, Mitch,'
he went on. 'You
know I hate for my
friends to avoid
me – if they owe
me money.

'*Especially* if
they owe me money.'

He smiled the kind
of smile only crocodiles
can manage.

It needs lots of teeth.

12

Mitch gulped. 'I'll pay you, Big Sid. Honest I will.'

He pointed to the poster on the wall. 'Knuckles Neddy is going to win big. He'll be Heavy-weight Champ. The prize is huge.'

Big Sid squinted at me.

'You think that elephant can beat Cool Vinny? Looks more like a punch-bag than a fighter.'

Me a punch-bag? I opened my mouth, then shut it. Fast.

'He's my top fighter. Best in the business. The prize is as good as ours. And you'll get every cent back.'

'Hasn't done much lately, has he?' snarled Big Sid.

'Tactics. We've been keeping him under wraps for the big one.'

'You gotta deal, monkey. I'll stretch the deadline. But if you don't pay up, at the ring, after the fight, *it's curtains!* That's a promise. You know I like to keep my promises.'

'Sure, Big Sid,' quavered Mitch as, jaws snapping, the croc disappeared.

I was shaking like a leaf.

'Mitch,' I yelled at him. 'You're depending on *me* to save you. You know Cool Vinny will murder me.'

Mitch wasn't listening. 'You worry too much, that's your trouble. Always has been. Something will turn up. Always does!'

I knew what would turn up! Big Sid and The Scaly Gang and a nice line in concrete over-shoes.

3 One-Pocket Pete

But something did turn up. He blew in the very next day.

A great big loping animal with enormous hind legs and tiny arms.

'Howdy, folk,' he said. 'Meet One-Pocket Pete. From Down Under. Beat everything on two and four legs down there. Want to clean up here. Looking for a smart manager.

'What's the form here? When do I start? Tomorrow's too late.'

'You're a boxer?' croaked Mitch.

The hat, which was hung around with corks, bounced up and down.

'Float like a bee. Sting like a butterfly – that's me.'

'You mean "Float like a butterfly, sting like a bee."'

'That's it, folk. That's what I said.'

Did this guy understand English?

All the time he bouncing around, fists up. Left hooks. Right jabs.

Mitch looked stunned. 'We're
saved!' he whispered. 'One-Pocket
Pete. Next champ of the Jungle. He'll
lick Cool Vinny. Let's put him
through his paces.'

Well, we tried.

We made him try press-ups, sit-
ups, jump-ups and pull-ups.

All we got was foul-ups, mess-ups,
screw-ups and cock-ups.

But, boy, did he try!

I was worn out looking at him.

He tried so hard that he wrapped himself around the ropes of the boxing-ring. He hung there panting.

'How did I do?' he wheezed when he got his breath back.

See what I mean. Rocky, he wasn't. That guy was bottoms. Lucky he had a pouch. He could climb into it and hide if a fight got too rough.

I couldn't believe my ears when
Mitch said, 'You're in! You fight
Cool Vinny the Lion on Saturday.'
My jaw dropped.

'Whaddaya mean he's fighting Cool
Vinny,' I shouted. 'That kangaroo
couldn't fight his way out of a paper
bag. He'll be eaten alive.'

Mitch just winked at me. 'Gotta
plan. Shhh! I'll tell you later.'

But Pete had heard us talking.

'I'm no paper bag, mate!' he cried, hopping up and down. 'I'm gonna be Champ. I'll pummel Cool Vinny like I was a jack-hammer. I'm gonna romp. I'm gonna stomp.'

He tried to slap his boxing gloves together, missed and boxed both his own ears. Then he collapsed in a heap. He was out for the count!

What a dumb animal!

It might be best if Cool Vinny put him out of his misery.

It was time for a heart-to-heart with Mitch.

'What's going on?' I asked. 'You know that dumb cluck hasn't a chance against Cool Vinny.'

Mitch was at the TV. 'Knuckles,' he cut in, 'remember that fox I know at Jungle TV. Well, watch this.'

He flicked on the set. It was just in time for the sports news. A sharp-looking fox came on screen.

'Attention, viewers. This is Digger Fox with an important news flash. Knuckles Neddy will *not* be fighting Cool Vinny in Saturday's big fight.

'He has an ingrown toenail, pretty serious when you think of the size of an elephant's toenail...ha! ha! ha!

'But boxing manager, Mitch the Monkey, has a secret weapon up his sleeve. At least it would be up his sleeve, if he had any...ha! ha! ha!...

'The secret weapon is One-Pocket Pete, the biggest thing since the Atomic Bomb. He'll make mince-meat of Cool Vinny. That's our top tip today … and, remember, folks, you heard it on this show first...

'Now to stool-pigeon racing...'

'That kangaroo,' I yelled at Mitch, 'is not an atom bomb. He's a soggy Christmas cracker.'

'I know, I know! One-Pocket Pete will be on the floor in ten seconds flat...*but we're going to bet all our money on Cool Vinny.* See?'

4 Big Sid Again

Just as a light was looming at the end of the tunnel, a shadow fell across the doorway. Big Sid!

Two visits in two days! You want to be a real popular kind of guy to expect to have the 'Welcome' mat rolled out again so soon. And Big Sid wasn't your average popular guy.

Behind him were two members of The Scaly Gang. Charlie, a state-of-the-art sap, and another sidekick.

The only pretty face was Peaches, Big Sid's girl-friend. She was class.

I think she had a soft spot for elephants. Especially me.

I didn't at first notice Slither Bob, the Hit-Snake – he has this habit of slithering in unnoticed. The first time you know he's there is when you drop dead. He does all Big Sid's dirty work with his poison fangs.

'Hiya, Big Sid,' quavered Mitch. 'Good to see ya.'

Big Sid gave a smile like death warmed up.

'What's this I'm hearing about Knuckles here and his ingrowing toenail. When did this happen?'

'You had just left yesterday,' said Mitch, 'when Knuckles here collapsed to the ground. "Mitch," he sobbed, "I can't move. My ingrowing..."'

'Spare me the gruesome details,' snapped Big Sid. 'You said yesterday Knuckles would make mince-meat of Cool Vinny. I was gonna put a stack on him. Then I heard Digger Fox.

'Now you have a *new* champ. And *he's* gonna make mince-meat of Cool Vinny. And you never told me!'

He sounded real sad.

'I meant to ring you,' said Mitch.

'Well, now, ain't that something. You know I hate for people for to keep me in the dark. Only for Digger Fox, I'd have been heavy into buckle Knuckles here...anyway, where's this Atomic Bomb?'

I pointed to One-Pocket Pete who was slumped on his stool, muttering to himself. He'd really creased himself the day before with that sucker punch.

'Doesn't look up to much.'

One-Pocket Pete jumped to his feet. 'You watch your mouth, Croc, he shouted, bouncing about. 'I'm the best roo in the business. I'm gonna sting like a butterfly, float like a bee. I'm gonna make Cool Vinny wish he'd been born a pussy cat.'

He was so excited that he gave an extra big bounce. Too high!

His dumb head whacked off the ceiling. He fell in a heap.

'I...I...I could have been Champ,' he croaked. Then he passed out.

Big Sid turned his battery of teeth on poor Mitch.

'Anything you wanna say? Like how atomic this damp squib is.'

'But he's perfect,' purred Peaches in her husky voice. 'That chump will never be champ. Let Mitch keep telling the media he's the greatest, blah, blah, blah... Everyone will back him – *and we'll be on Cool Vinny!*'

'You're one helluva smart dame,' said Big Sid. 'You hear that, Mitch. Go big on the media. But keep the dope out of sight until the big night. And zip your lips. Not a word to anyone – especially not the Gorilla Twins. Or you'll end up wearing concrete over-shoes. You gotta a note of all that, Charlie.'

Charlie was paring his pencil.

Peaches gave me a big smile.

'I'll be *awfully* grateful to you if Cool Vinny wins,' she purred.

I blushed to the end of my trunk.

Big Sid's eyes glinted nastily. 'Keep your eyes off my dame, Knuckles,' he snarled. 'And just make sure that kangaroo doesn't get lucky.'

Jaws snapping, they disappeared.

5 The Gorilla Twins

'So,' said Mitch, 'he wants One-Pocket Pete to take a dive. That's OK by us, isn't it? So do we.'

Had that chimp no heart?

One-Pocket Pete was still flat out on the canvas. I got a bucket of water and threw it over him.

He sat up spluttering.

'Whassup!' he said, rubbing the lump on his head. 'Did I win?'

Was this dummy for real? I gave him a fluffy towel and told him to take a hot shower.

'AM I CHAMP?'

As he staggered off, Mitch did a little jig. He was singing 'Money! Money! Money!'

My mind was on concrete shoes.

'I hope One-Pocket doesn't go and do something like winning,' I said.

'But dat's just wot he's goin' to do, ain't it?' rumbled a very deep voice.

It was Bash, one of the Gorilla Twins. Boy, were they tough cookies! How much had they heard?

'Right on, Bash,' said Smash, the other half. He chewed on a fat cigar.

'Dat kangarrooo is gonna pummel Cool Vinny. That way, we win lots of lovely dosh.'

Mitch was speechless.

'But...he's no good,' he stuttered. 'He can't fight. He can't win!

Smash dropped his cigar.

'Whaddaya mean? Of course he's gonna win. Digger Fox says so. And it's all over de papers today.'

He produced several chewed-up bits of paper from his pockets.

He was right. It's all over the papers.

OZZIE LEGEND HITS JUNGLE

WILL VINNY LAST ROUND ONE?

SUPER KANGA TO K.O. VINNY

'That's what the story is,' said Bash.
'They're all wrong,' quaked Mitch.

'Know what I think, Bash.'
'Spill it, Smash?'
'I tink dis ere pair want to keep dis ere kangarrooo under wraps. Tellin' us he's no good when he's gonna K.O. Cool Vinny in two seconds flat.'
'Why don't you bet on the sure thing...Cool Vinny?' I said.

'Nah,' drawled Smash. 'We like *our* idea better. We hear Big Sid is gonna put his shirt on him. So, if Cool Vinny loses, Big Sid loses. *All* his money. We'll be the biggest gangsters in the Jungle. Right, Bash?'

'Right on, Smash!' said Bash.

'If that kangarrooo *doesn't* win,' said Smash, 'I'll suspect dirty work. You pair better get your act together. Udderwise, you might both end up gettin' stuffed and hung up on de wall at de Gangster Club.'

'Why don't we have a look at the champ?' said Bash.

Mitch pointed towards the shower. The gorillas peered into the steam.

They could see nothing because of the clouds of steam. But they could hear One-Pocket Pete hollering the old Ozzie song: *'Walzin' Aunt Hilda...Walzin' Aunt Hilda...Who'll go a'walzin' Aunt Hilda with meeee!'*

'Sounds fine to me,' said Bash.

'Like he had it all wrapped up,' said Smash.

The heavyweight pair turned and pounded out.

Mitch and I looked at each other.

If One-Pocket Pete *won* the fight, we'd end up at the bottom of the river wearing concrete over-shoes.

If he *lost*, we'd get stuffed and put up on the wall at the Gangster Club.

It didn't take a genius to sum up.

We were skating on thin ice.

6 The Big Fight

When we arrived for the fight, we could hardly get to the ring.

The whole jungle was there, pushing and shoving, snarling and roaring, fighting to get the best seats.

Four big coconut trees marked out the ring. Two rows of rope hung between them to keep the fighters IN – and the crowd OUT.

The Gorilla Twins were in the front row, surrounded by 'minders' –

baboons, orang-utans and gibbons.

The Scaly Gang were also in the front row – on the other side. They all wore bow ties, even Peaches. She looked a real dish.

I didn't say Hello. I had other things to think about. Like getting stuffed or fitted for concrete shoes.

Half-Eye Hippo was the referee. He had a black patch over one eye and squinted badly out of the other.

Nobody knew how he got to be referee. It was wiser not to ask.

He raised a hoof for silence.

'Friends and Fowl, Birds and Beasts. Welcome all. In the red corner...the coolest cat of them all...the champ of the Deep Dark Jungle...Cooool Vinneee the Lion!!!'

From the corner of the ring came a mighty roar. All the big cats – spotty leopards, laughing hyenas and slinky panthers – were there to support him.

In swaggered the fearsome champ, wearing dark sun-glasses and a leather jacket. He gave a long purr and began to slick back his furry mane with a steel comb.

'Don't mind who I beat up,' he roared, 'just as long as they're tasty!!'

'And in the blue corner,' went on the hippo, 'trained by the mighty Knuckles Neddy...the dark horse... the fighter with the punch of an Atomic Bomb...it's One-Pocket Peeeete, the kangaroooooo!!!'

One-Pocket Pete waved his fists in the air and danced about.

The giraffes, zebras and all the deer family, safely out of reach of the big cats, went wild. They didn't like lions one little bit.

Above the ring, perched the vultures. They didn't care who won the fight as long as they got to take a peck out of the loser.

I must say Pete really looked the part. He wore a natty cloak with a big hood and his best boxing gloves.

The words 'One-Pocket Rocket' were written in big gold letters on the back of the cloak.

The only problem was that the hood had got tangled over his eyes and he couldn't pull it free. He lurched from side to side.

Could he get *anything* right?

'Ere, steady on, young feller,' grumbled Half-Eye Hippo. 'Take off that hood. We're starting.'

He rang a loud bell.

JANGALANGALNANG!!

The fight was on.

As you probably know, most fights follow a pattern. First, both boxers start circling. Some light jabbing goes on as they test each other. Then one of them throws a knockout punch.

And all hell breaks loose.

One fighter has his arms in the air.

The other lies on the canvas with a lot of teeth missing.

The winner gets a wreath or a cup. The loser gets to the medical centre.

That wasn't quite how this fight went. Mainly because One-Pocket Pete, vainly trying to fix his hood, still couldn't see a thing.

'Come on out. Where are you hiding?' he shouted at Cool Vinny.

Cool Vinny banged his gloves and made straight for Pete.

7 Knock-Outs!

I'm not usually a queasy kind of guy
but I shut my eyes. This was going to
be a massacre.

'Oh, why did I do this to that poor
dumb kangaroo?' Mitch moaned.

About time he thought of that!

Suddenly I felt something being
pressed into my hoof. What was it?

It was a note!

It read: 'Knuckles. Be ready to take
action. You must stop the fight now.
Signed: A friend.'

A dainty little paw print was
smudged at the bottom. Was it...?
There was no time to work it out.

'Come on, Mitch,' I cried. 'It's now
or never for you and me.'

In the ring things were going from bad to worse. One-Pocket Pete still hadn't got free of the hood.

First he smacked into a tree.

Cool Vinny was holding his sides.

'Over here,' he chortled. 'Whenever you find the time.'

The crowd were starting to boo.

'I have you now, Lion,' huffed One-Pocket Pete, flapping his fists at Half-Eye Hippo. He pulled back his fist and WHACK.

He hit him right on the nose.

Due to his eye-patch getting in his line of vision, the hippo didn't know where the punch had come from.

'Ere, that's not in the rules.' He squinted at Cool Vinny. 'Take that!'

He stuck out a hoof and smacked Cool Vinny.

'Oi,' shouted Vinny. He was mad. 'There seem to be three of us in this fight. It's getting a bit crowded!'

Then he swung both fists.

BIFF! BAM!

He thumped Half-Eye Hippo and One-Pocket Pete with two corkers.

The three animals rolled about the ring in a big angry ball.

Oooff! Ooooww!! Eeeeekk!!! Kerrsplatt!!!!

The crowd loved it. Dust and fists and gloves were everywhere. Fights broke out all over the place.

This was my chance. It was a long time since I had fought Cool Vinny but an elephant never forgets.

I hadn't forgotten that weak spot!

I sneaked around the ring and waited until his head popped up. I didn't need to be asked twice.

I bopped Cool Vinny clean out of it with a beauty of a right hook. Down he went like a sack of spuds.

K.O. in one hit!

One-Pocket Pete and Half-Eye Hippo were still moshing about in the middle of the ring.

Not for long!

Mitch shimmied up a nearby tree. A huge coconut came crashing down into the ring.

OOF! It smacked One-Pocket Pete right on the noggin. He collapsed in a heap.

K.O. number 2 and right on time.

Half-Eye Hippo just couldn't
work out what was going on.

With his half-eye, he squinted at
the fallen bodies of Cool Vinny and
One-Pocket Pete.

'Wot's going on?' he sniffed,
rubbing his eye patch. 'This ain't in
the rules. Someone is supposed to
stay standing. I declare this fight null
and void. All bets are off.'

Uproar from the crowd!

The Scaly Gang and the Gorilla Twins looked mad as hell. They made straight for Mitch and me.

Big Sid grabbed Mitch and shook him. He was raging mad. 'All my money,' he roared. 'All gone. It's concrete shoes for both of you.'

Then Bash and Smash lumbered up. They pinned my arms.

'In a while, crocodile,' shouted Bash. 'We're gonna stuff these jokers!'

Suddenly Peaches appeared. With a big wink at me, she popped a pair of handcuffs on Big Sid.

'I'm Special Agent Peaches McGraw. I work undercover with JAB – the Jungle Assets Bureau. I pretended to be Big Sid's girl-friend to get proof that he has been using Offshore Bank Accounts to run his gambling racket.'

So, *she* had written the note.

'Big Sid is under arrest and so are all the Scaly Gang,' she said sternly.

Big Sid nearly swallowed his teeth.

'Dames! You can't trust them!' he growled. 'But you won't get me. Charlie, I hope you're making a note of all this. And get me my lawyer.'

'He's in jail,' said Peaches sweetly.

'Where the Gorilla Twins are about to join him,' a voice said.

A big black horse wearing a police helmet crashed through the trees.

'I'm Sergeant Stallion of the Special Branch,' he announced. 'I'm arresting Bash and Smash.'

'What's the rap?' growled Bash.

'On suspicion of rigging this boxing match – and smoking cigars in the No Smoking section.'

Bash and Smash were as choked as chimneys.

'We wuz only tryin' to get a little money for the Christmas,' sniffed Bash.

'We didn't mean no harm,' sobbed Smash.

Then Sergeant Stallion led the Gorilla Twins and The Scaly Gang off to the cells.

'Nice one, Sarge,' smiled Peaches.

8 After the Fight

What happened *après* (as they say in France)?

Cool Vinny was lifted out of the ring by giraffe crane. The lump on his head hasn't gone down yet.

One-Pocket Pete keeps on about fighting Cool Vinny all over again. That knock on the head must have scrambled what was left of his brains.

Half-Eye Hippo doesn't referee
any more. Says it's too dangerous.
He's now into surf boarding.

Mitch and I threw a party at The
Swinging Vine.

Peaches came and said she knew
she could rely on us to help. She's
agreed to have dinner with me –
when she's not on duty with JAB,
that is.

The baddies are still in jail. All the
money they made illegally was taken
from them. They'll have to work
when they get out – if they ever do.

Although the jungle is now a safer place to live in, Mitch and I have decided to retire to a nice little cottage with roses around the door, far from the jungle's roar.

As a start, I've written out a nice big sign which I've just put up outside The Swinging Vine:

FOR SALE — TWO BOXING GLOVES — ALMOST NEW -- ONE CAREFUL OWNER — BEST OFFER SECURES.

PAINT

A little about Elephants

Someone wrote to ask me why I gave information on *elephants* at the end of *The Hungry Horse*, which was about a horse.

It's because it belongs to the **Elephant** series – books that are easy and fun to read with lots of pictures. And at the end of each book, I tell you a little about elephants.

This is **Elephant No. 4** and by chance the hero *is* an elephant – Knuckles Neddy.

He says somewhere: 'An elephant never forgets.' Is that true?

It really is! People who study elephants say we are quick to learn, mainly because we remember things from the past.

For instance, if there is no water in one place, we remember where it is and how to get to it.

We never forget!

A Little about Speaking

Some people have a very odd way of saying what they mean.

Take Big Sid.

He wants to say, 'I hate people to keep me in the dark.' Instead he says, 'I hate *for* people *for* to keep me in the dark.'

That's his way of speaking – but don't copy! He can be hard to understand.

One-Pocket Pete, too, is often hard to understand.

'Whassup?' he says. He means, 'What is up?' or 'What's up?' But he slurs the words together.

The Gorilla Twins aren't much better. They say 'dat' for 'that', 'wot' for 'what' and 'dis' for 'this'.

But they, unlike you and me, probably never went to school and were never taught to speak clearly.

Elephants – easy reading for new readers who have moved on a stage. Still with –

> Large type
> Mostly short words
> Short sentences
> Lots of illustrations
> And great fun!

There are now four **Elephants**:

1. *The True Story of the Three Little Pigs and the Big Bad Wolf*
2. *The Hungry Horse*
3. *The Trial of the Big Bad Wolf*
4. *Jitters in the Jungle*

Noel Ward lives in the seaside town of Skerries in County Dublin. When not writing about Knuckles Neddy and his friends, he works as a reporter in Dáil Eireann in Leinster House, Dublin.

Jitters in the Jungle is his first book for children. However, in spite of being locked up in jail at the moment, Big Sid and the Gorilla Twins may surface in another 'jungle' adventure.

Terry Myler, one of Ireland's best-known illustrators, has worked on all four **Elephant** books. She has also written two books which are essential for budding artists: *Drawing Made Easy* and *Drawing Made Very Easy*.